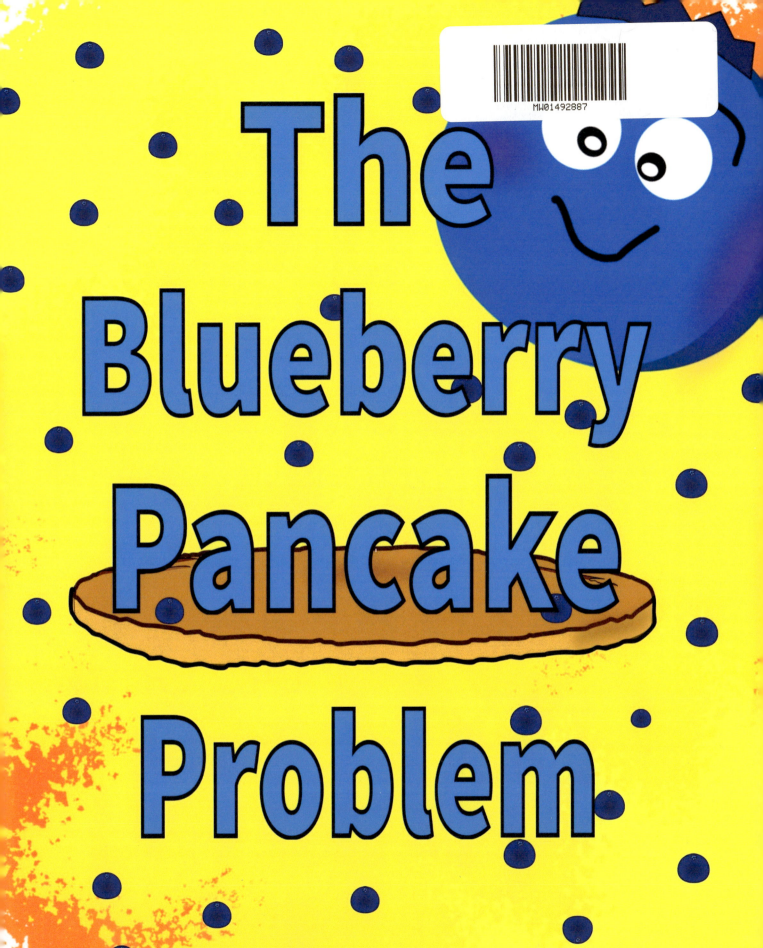

The Blueberry Pancake Problem

For teaching resources:

Visit us at MakingTheBasicsFun.com

ISBN: 0-9989992-0-2

ISBN-13: 978-0-9989992-0-3

By Angela Kantorowicz

Illustrated by Angela and Grace Kantorowicz

2017©

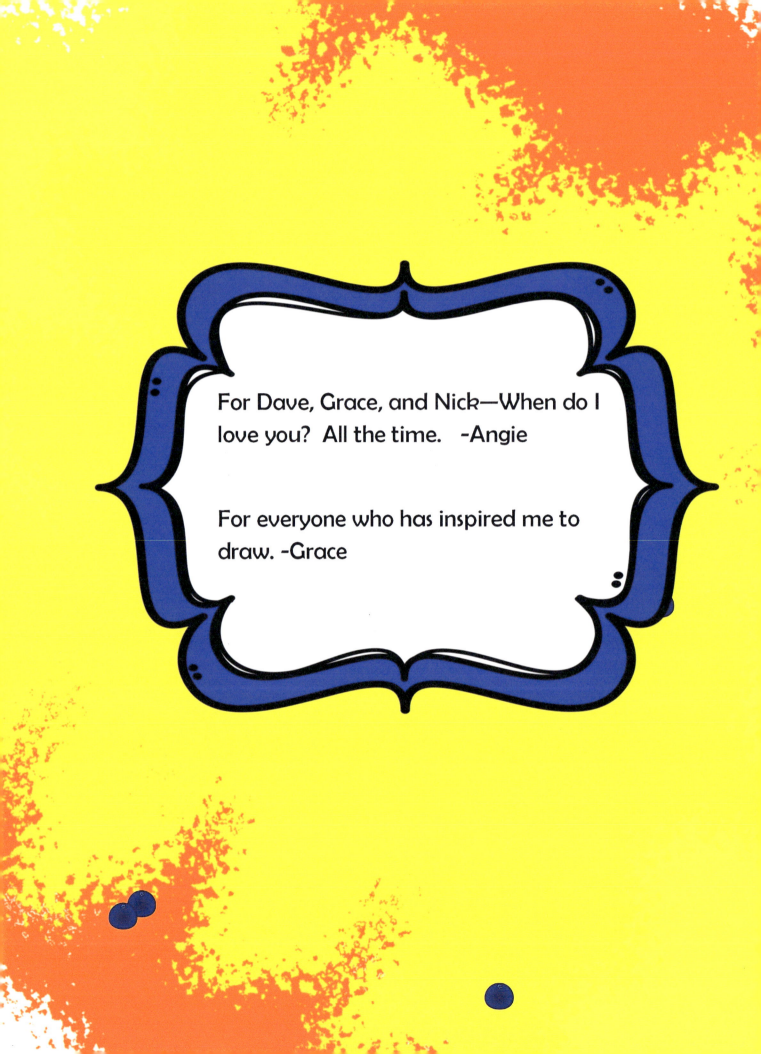

For Dave, Grace, and Nick—When do I love you? All the time.   -Angie

For everyone who has inspired me to draw. -Grace

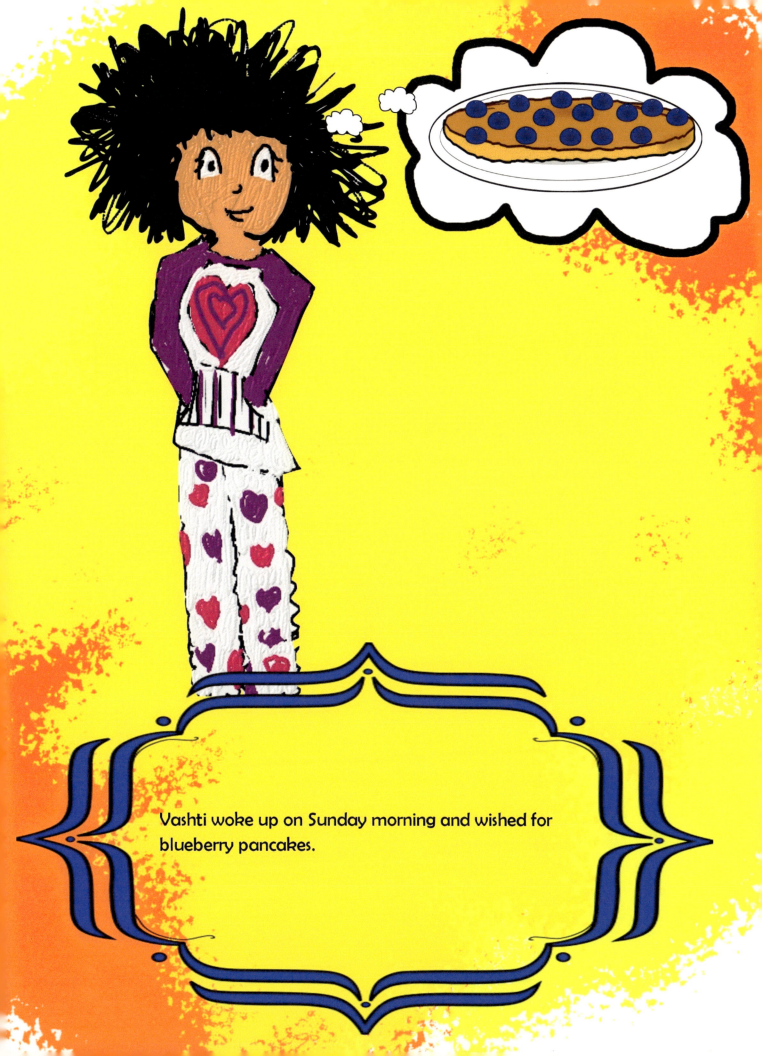

Vashti woke up on Sunday morning and wished for blueberry pancakes.

She ran into the kitchen to see her dad mixing up pancake batter.

"Good morning Vashti!" said Vashti's dad. "You're just in time to help me make pancakes."

"Are we having pancakes with strawberries and whipped cream?" asked Vashti.

"Nope," said Vashti's dad.

"Are we having pancakes with bananas and peanut butter?" asked Vashti.

"Not this time," said Vashti's dad.

"Are we having pancakes with blueberries?" asked Vashti.

"Yepper doodle!" smiled Vashti's dad. "And you get to put as many blueberries on your pancake as you want. But remember, you are what you eat, so don't eat too many blueberries, or you might turn into a blueberry."

Vashti took a handful of plump, juicy blueberries and put them on her pancake. She counted them one by one.

"One, two, three, four, five."

"Five blueberries doesn't look like enough blueberries," thought Vashti.

So she put another handful of blueberries on her pancake. She continued counting.

"Let's see, I had five blueberries, now I have six, seven, eight, nine, ten."

"Ten blueberries still doesn't look like enough blueberries," thought Vashti.

So she put another handful of blueberries on her pancake, and continued counting.

"Let's see, I had 10 blueberries, now I have eleven, twelve, thirteen, fourteen, fifteen."

"Fifteen blueberries looks just right," thought Vashti.

She grabbed her fork and ate her pancake with 15 blueberries, in 15 seconds flat.

"Holy smoly!" said Vashti's dad.

"You must be really hungry. Would you like a second pancake?"

"Yepper doodle!" smiled Vashti.

"Here's your second pancake. You get to put as many blueberries on your pancake as you want. But remember, you are what you eat, so don't eat too many blueberries, or you might turn into a blueberry."

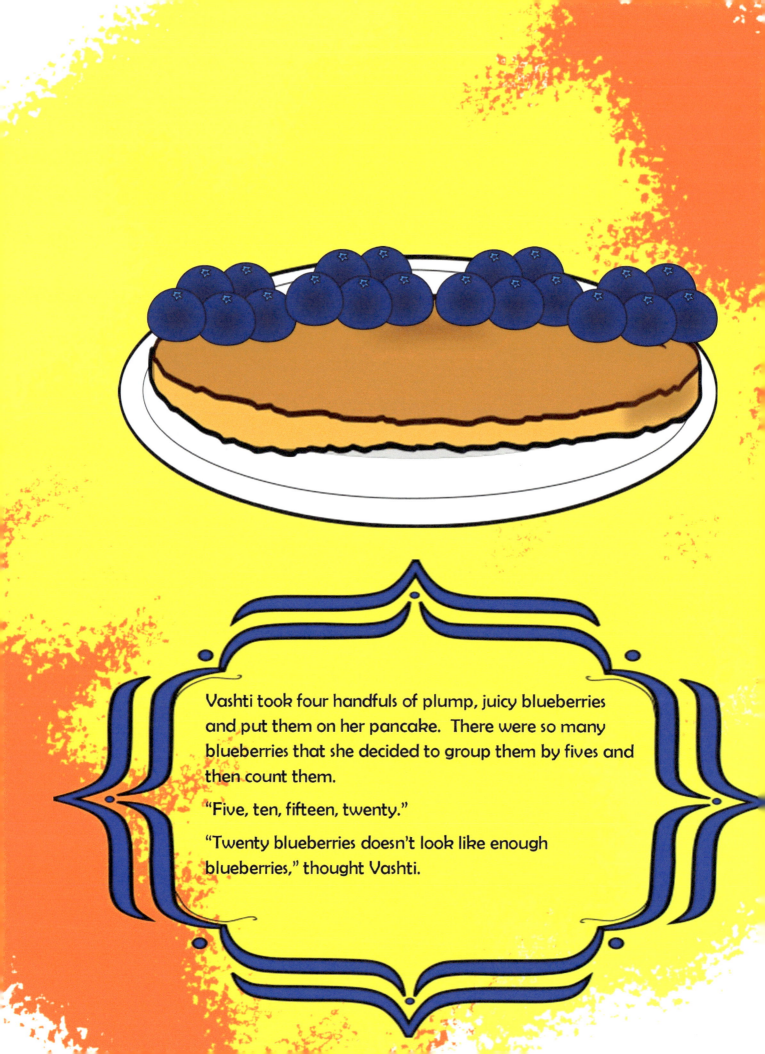

Vashti took four handfuls of plump, juicy blueberries and put them on her pancake. There were so many blueberries that she decided to group them by fives and then count them.

"Five, ten, fifteen, twenty."

"Twenty blueberries doesn't look like enough blueberries," thought Vashti.

So she put four more handfuls of blueberries on her pancake. She continued grouping and counting by fives.

"Let's see, I had twenty blueberries, now I have twenty-five, thirty, thirty-five, forty."

"Forty blueberries still doesn't look like enough blueberries," thought Vashti.

So she put four more handfuls of blueberries on her pancake. She continued grouping and counting by fives.

"Let's see, I had forty blueberries, now I forty-five, fifty, fifty-five, sixty."

"Sixty blueberries looks just right," thought Vashti.

She grabbed her fork and ate her second pancake with sixty blueberries, in sixty seconds flat.

"Holy schmoly olie!" said Vashti's dad.

"You must be really, really hungry. Would you like a third pancake?"

"Yepper doodle!" smiled Vashti.

"Here's your third pancake. You get to put as many blueberries on your pancake as you want. But remember, you are what you eat, so don't eat too many blueberries, or you might turn into a blueberry."

Vashti took seven handfuls of plump, juicy blueberries and put them on her pancake. She continued grouping and counting her blueberries by fives.

"Five, ten, fifteen, twenty, twenty-five, thirty, thirty-five."

"Thirty-five blueberries doesn't look like enough blueberries," thought Vashti.

So she put seven more handfuls on her pancake. She continued to group and count the blueberries by fives.

"Let's see, I had thirty-five blueberries, now I have forty, forty-five, fifty, fifty-five, sixty, sixty-five, seventy.

"Seventy blueberries still doesn't look like enough blueberries," thought Vashti.

So she put seven more handfuls on her pancake. She continued to group and count the blueberries by fives.

"Let's see, I had seventy blueberries, now I have seventy-five, eighty, eighty-five, ninety, ninety-five, one hundred, ONE HUNDRED FIVE!"

"One hundred five blueberries looks just right," thought Vashti.

And she ate her third pancake with one hundred five blueberries in 105 seconds flat.

Just then, Vashti began to feel a gurgle in her toes and hear a ringing in her ears. She looked at her hands and they were plump and blue.

"Oh no," groaned Vashti. "I think I ate too many blueberries."

15

60

105

"Vashti?" whispered Vashti's dad. "Did you eat more than 15 blueberries?"

"Yes," whispered Vashti.

"Vashti?" groaned Vashti's dad. "Did you eat more than sixty blueberries?"

"Yes," moaned Vashti.

"Vashti!" panicked Vashti's dad. "Did you eat more than 105 blueberries?"

"Yepper Doodle," confessed Vashti.

"Vashti, how many blueberries did you eat?"

Vashti wanted to cry, but right in front of her was a plain pancake dripping in butter and maple syrup. It looked so good; she just had to have bite. She ate her fourth pancake in ten seconds flat.

Then, she felt a gurgle in her ears, and a ringing in her toes. Vashti looked at her fingers as the purple color began to disappear.

"Vashti!" said Vashti's dad. "Hurry, eat another plain pancake."

So Vashti ate her fifth, sixth, seventh, eighth, ninth, and tenth plain pancake in sixty seconds flat.

"Vashti!" said Vashti's dad. "All of those plain pancakes have turned you back into your plain self. I must have been right. You are what you eat."

The next Sunday morning, Vashti didn't wake up
wishing for blueberry pancakes. Instead, she wished for
blueberry waffles with whipped cream.

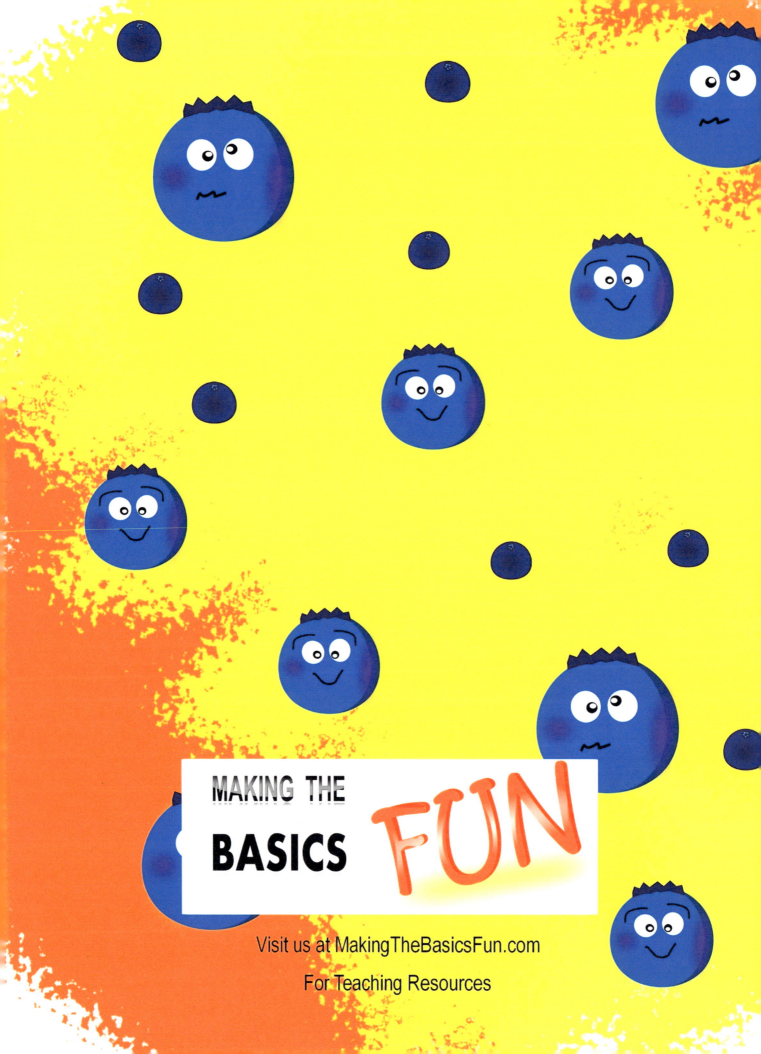

MAKING THE BASICS FUN

Visit us at MakingTheBasicsFun.com

For Teaching Resources

Made in United States
Troutdale, OR
08/31/2024

22485238R00021